Mrs. Boot
the farmer,

four geese

and a duck.

Poppy and Sam were
very excited.

Today was market day.

Mrs. Boot put the trailer on the car.

And off they went.

The market was full of noisy animals.

"I like the cows best,"
said Sam.

Mooo!

"Let's look at the birds,"
said Mrs. Boot.

They looked in all
the cages.

"I like those white
geese," said Mrs. Boot.

"Let's buy them."

Ducklings!

"Look," said Poppy.
"There's a lonely duck."

"I wish I could buy it."

Mrs. Boot didn't hear.
She was putting the
geese in a cage.

11

One goose flew out of
the cage.

It ran to a car.

The goose jumped in...

...and then jumped out the other side!

"I'll get the naughty
goose!" cried Sam.

At last, they caught
the goose.

"Will you come and see a duck?" asked Poppy. "I'd like to buy it."

"It's lovely," said
Mrs. Boot.

"Now it won't be
lonely," said Poppy.

"Time to go home,"
said Mrs. Boot.

"I have my geese."

"And I have my very
own duck," said Poppy.

PUZZLES

Puzzle 1

Ṫrue or false?

A.

There are two ducklings.

B.

The duck is black.

C.

The geese are in the cage.

D.

I have my very own pig.

E.

One goose flew out.

Puzzle 2

Find these things in the picture.

dog   kitten   trailer

hens   car   cage

Puzzle 3

Can you spot five differences between these two pictures?

Puzzle 4

Choose a word from the box to fill in the gap in each sentence.

lonely   cages

noisy   geese

A.

What a lot of _____ animals.

B.

They looked in all the _____.

C.

That duck looks _____.

D.

I have my _____.

Answers to puzzles

Puzzle 1

True

A.

There are two ducklings.

False

B.

The duck is black.

True

C.

The geese are in the cage.

False

D.

I have my very own pig

True

E.

One goose flew out.

Puzzle 2

dog

car

cage

trailer

hens

kitten

Puzzle 3

Puzzle 4

A. What a lot of <u>noisy</u> animals.

B. They looked in all the <u>cages</u>.

C. That duck looks <u>lonely</u>.

D. I have my <u>geese</u>.

Designed by Laura Nelson
Series editor: Lesley Sims
Series designer: Russell Punter
Digital manipulation by Nick Wakeford

This edition first published in 2016 by Usborne Publishing Ltd.,
Usborne House, 83-85 Saffron Hill, London EC1N 8RT, England.
www.usborne.com Copyright © 2016, 1989 Usborne Publishing Ltd.

USBORNE FIRST READING
Level Two

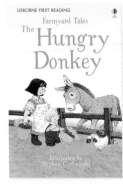
Farmyard Tales
The Hungry Donkey
Illustrated by Stephen Cartwright

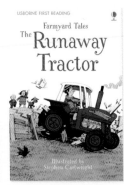
Farmyard Tales
The Runaway Tractor
Illustrated by Stephen Cartwright

Farmyard Tales
The Naughty Sheep
Illustrated by Stephen Cartwright

Farmyard Tales
Tractor in Trouble
Illustrated by Stephen Cartwright

Farmyard Tales
Scarecrow's Secret
Illustrated by Stephen Cartwright

Farmyard Tales
The New Pony
Illustrated by Stephen Cartwright

Farmyard Tales
Pig Gets Lost
Illustrated by Stephen Cartwright

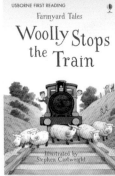
Farmyard Tales
Woolly Stops the Train
Illustrated by Stephen Cartwright

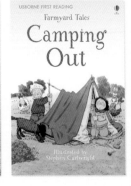
Farmyard Tales
Camping Out
Illustrated by Stephen Cartwright